W9-APL-668

An I Can Read Book™

Inspector Hopper's Mystery Year

story and pictures by

Doug Cushman

HarperCollins*Publishers*

To Maurice Sendak,
who taught us all what a book could be
—D.C.

HarperCollins®, ☕®, and I Can Read Book® are
trademarks of HarperCollins Publishers Inc.

Inspector Hopper's Mystery Year
Copyright © 2003 by Doug Cushman
Printed in the U.S.A. All rights reserved.
www.harperchildrens.com

Library of Congress Cataloging-in-Publication Data is available.
ISBN 0-06-008962-8 — ISBN 0-06-008963-6 (lib. bdg.)

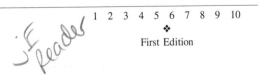

1 2 3 4 5 6 7 8 9 10
❖
First Edition

Contents

An Autumn Mystery

Emma Worm ran into the office

of Inspector Hopper, Private Bug.

"A ghost moved in next door!"

she cried.

"How do you know?"

asked Inspector Hopper.

"I heard a voice next door,

but the house is empty," said Emma.

"I do not believe in ghosts,"

said Inspector Hopper.

"Still, this is a mystery.

Please tell us more."

"I live in a pumpkin

at Miss Millie's Pumpkin Farm,"

said Emma.

"Last night someone was talking

inside the pumpkin next door.

But no one lives there.

The whole neighborhood is scared.

Please help us!"

"Let's go, McBugg!"

said Inspector Hopper.

"We have a mystery to solve!"

"I haven't finished my supper,"

said McBugg.

"Finish it later,"

said Inspector Hopper.

Inspector Hopper and McBugg

followed Emma to the pumpkin farm.

A cold wind rustled the trees.

Dry leaves crackled and crunched.

"It is very spooky here,"

said McBugg.

"I wonder if ghosts

really do live here."

"I do not believe in ghosts,"

said Inspector Hopper.

"This is my house," said Emma,

"and that is the haunted house."

"I don't hear anything," said McBugg.

Suddenly they heard

SLURP! CRUNCH!

"A ghost!" cried McBugg.

"OOHH!" said the pumpkin.

The pumpkin began to move.

CRUNCH! SLURP!

"YUMM!" said the pumpkin.

"The pumpkin is going to eat us!"

said McBugg.

"Help!" cried all the worms.

Inspector Hopper looked
all around the pumpkin.
"I don't see any footprints
around the pumpkin," he said.
"There are no clues
on the pumpkin, either.
But there *is* something inside."
"A ghost doesn't leave footprints,"
said McBugg.

Inspector Hopper thought for a moment.

He noticed a long mound of dirt

going to the pumpkin.

"I have an idea," he said.

Inspector Hopper began to dig

in the mound of dirt.

"Hello, hello!" he cried.

"Come out this way!"

"What is he doing?" asked Emma.

15

The mound of dirt

began to move.

Out popped . . . a gopher!

"Hello, Murray,"

said Inspector Hopper.

"I thought you might be stuck."

"I *was* stuck!" said Murray.

"I was digging in my tunnel.

This pumpkin was in the way.

So I began to eat it.

It was yummy.

Then I got stuck inside.

Thank you for digging me out."

"There is your ghost,"

said Inspector Hopper.

"The mound of dirt

was a good clue.

It made me think of a gopher.

You don't have to worry

about ghosts anymore."

"Thank you!" said Emma.

18

"Another case solved,"

said Inspector Hopper.

"I wonder what a house tastes like,"

said McBugg.

A Winter Mystery

"Achoo! Honk!"

Inspector Hopper blew his nose.

"I am so sick," he said.

"I can't do any

detective work today."

"You must go to the doctor,"

said McBugg.

"Here is your scarf.

I will go with you."

A cold wind blew around

the bugs' knees.

Snow whizzed by their heads.

"Achoo!" Inspector Hopper sneezed.

Inspector Hopper and McBugg

arrived at the doctor's office.

"Hello!" called McBugg.

No one was there.

"Maybe the doctor is out

helping other bugs," said McBugg.

"Yes," said Inspector Hopper.

"His doctor bag is always here.

Now it's gone."

"But his coat is still here,"
said McBugg.

"He would not go out into the snow
without his coat."

"Look!" said Inspector Hopper.

"Here is a cup of tea.

It is still hot!

Where could the doctor be?

This is a real mystery.

Let's look through the house

for more clues."

Inspector Hopper and McBugg

looked through the house.

They looked in the waiting room.

They looked

in the closets.

They looked in the kitchen.

They even looked in the bathroom.

But the doctor was not there.

Suddenly the two bugs heard

"Honk!"

"It's coming from the bedroom!"

said McBugg.

They ran into the bedroom.

A mysterious shape

moved under the covers.

"Stop!" cried Inspector Hopper.

"Where is the doctor?

Who are you?"

"Achoo! Honk!"

"Doctor!" said Inspector Hopper.

"I am so sick," said the doctor.

"I could not call out to you.

I brought my doctor bag in here

but I forgot my cup of tea.

I was too sick to get up again."

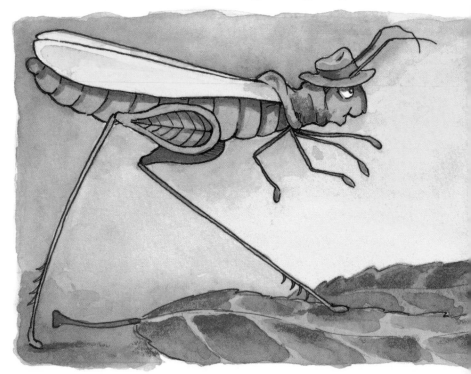

"Achoo!" said Inspector Hopper.

"I am sick, too."

"You need rest and hot tea,"

said the doctor.

McBugg made two cups of tea.

He helped Inspector Hopper

get under a blanket in a chair.

"It is no fun being sick,"

said Inspector Hopper,

"but it is good to be sick

with a friend."

"Honk! Achoo!" said the doctor.

A Spring Mystery

"I love hopping

through the tall grass

on a windy day like today,"

said Inspector Hopper.

"I like eating the tall grass

on a day like today," said McBugg.

"Inspector Hopper!"

a voice called out.

"Hello, Mrs. Beetle,"

said Inspector Hopper.

"What is wrong?"

"My little Miko is gone!" she cried.

35

"I called and called,"

said Mrs. Beetle,

"but Miko did not answer.

I am so worried."

"We will help you,"

said Inspector Hopper.

Inspector Hopper and McBugg

followed Mrs. Beetle.

"Miko was playing right here,"

she said.

"I went inside

to bring in some laundry.

I was only gone for a second.

When I came back, Miko was gone.

Where could she be?"

"The only clue I see

is this piece of string,"

said Inspector Hopper.

"That is not much help.

We need to find more clues.

Wait here, Mrs. Beetle."

"Look!" said McBugg.

"I see another clue."

"Paper and string,"

said Inspector Hopper.

"What kind of clues are these?"

Inspector Hopper and McBugg
hopped on through the tall grass.
"Oh, no!" cried McBugg.
"My hat blew off my head!"

He chased after his hat.

The hat went high into the air.

Then it fell into a puddle.

"Yuck!" said McBugg.

"My hat is soaking wet."

Inspector Hopper laughed.

"You should tie a string to your hat

so it won't blow away."

Inspector Hopper stopped.

"Wait!" he said.

"I have an idea.

What can you do with some string

and some paper on a windy day?"

"Make a hat?" said McBugg.

"Maybe," said Inspector Hopper.

"But what else?"

McBugg thought for a minute.

"I know!" he said at last.

"You need string, paper,

and a windy day to fly a kite!"

"Yes!" said Inspector Hopper.

"And I know the best place

to fly a kite.

Follow me!"

McBugg followed Inspector Hopper

to a big hill.

On top of the hill

were many bugs flying kites.

One bug was tangled

in some string around a flower.

It was Miko.

"Help!" she cried.

Inspector Hopper and McBugg

untangled the string.

"I was too tangled to move,"

said Miko,

"and it was so windy,

the other bugs

couldn't hear me calling."

"Go on home now,"

said Inspector Hopper.

"Thank you!" said Miko.

"Another mystery solved,"

said Inspector Hopper.

"Let's fly a kite!" said McBugg.

Squish went McBugg's hat.

47

A Summer Mystery

Inspector Hopper and McBugg

hopped through the tall grass.

"Listen!" said McBugg.

"I hear someone crying."

"Over there!" said Inspector Hopper.

"Hello, Holly Cricket," said McBugg.

"Why are you crying?"

"Someone has stolen my music!"

said Holly.

"I was singing a new song
with my group the Crickets,"
said Holly.
"We went out for lunch.
When we returned,
the music was gone!
We must have it
for our show tonight."

Inspector Hopper looked around.

"I don't see any clues," he said.

"No mounds of dirt,

no scraps of paper, no strings.

Nothing!"

"It's almost as if

the thief flew in from the sky,"

said McBugg.

"Maybe the thief *did* have wings,"

said Inspector Hopper.

He looked up.

He saw a line of geese in the sky.

"Birds have wings," he said.

"Let's go to the pond

and talk to the geese."

Inspector Hopper, McBugg, and Holly

hopped down to the pond.

"Hello, geese," said Inspector Hopper.

"We are looking for

some missing music.

Can you help us?"

"We don't need any music!"

cried the geese.

"We already know how to sing.

HONK! HONK! HONK!"

"I don't think they have a clue,"

said Inspector Hopper.

"My ears hurt," said McBugg.

"Who else has wings?"

asked Inspector Hopper.

"Bats have wings," said McBugg.

"Great idea," said Inspector Hopper.

"Let's talk to the bats."

Inspector Hopper, McBugg, and Holly

hopped to a cave.

"Hello!"

called Inspector Hopper.

"We are looking

for some missing music.

Can you help us?"

"We are trying to sleep!"

cried the bats.

"Don't you know

it's the middle of the day?

Go away or we will eat you!"

"Run!" said Inspector Hopper.

"Who else has wings?"

asked Holly.

BUZZ! BUZZ!

Inspector Hopper looked up.

Overhead was a wasp's nest.

"Wasps have wings," he said.

"Let's ask Franklin Wasp."

Inspector Hopper, McBugg, and Holly
climbed the tree.

They looked at the nest.

In the middle of the nest
was a sheet of music.

"My music!" cried Holly.

"Hello, everyone," said Franklin.

"What brings you to my nest?"

"A mystery," said Inspector Hopper.

"Where did you find

this piece of music?"

"Is that music?" asked Franklin.

"I found it near the Cricket Club.

It looked like old scrap paper.

I needed something

to patch a hole in my nest.

I did not know it was music."

"It's mine," said Holly.

"I need it for my show tonight."

"But without this paper

I will have a big hole in my nest!"

said Franklin. "What can I do?"

"I have an idea," said Inspector Hopper,

"but we will need some strong bugs."

That night at the Cricket Club

there was Franklin's nest onstage!

"I present to you my buddy,

Holly, and the Crickets!"

said Franklin.

Holly and the Crickets began to sing.

They could see the music.

Everyone was happy.

"Another case solved,"

said Inspector Hopper.

The two detectives hopped

into the tall grass

while the Crickets' music played

far into the summer night.